Island of the Unicorn

JEAN «MOEBIUS» GIRAUD
MARC BATI
co-creators
RANDY & JEAN-MARC LOFFICIER
translators
BERND METZ
JEAN-JACQUES SURBECK
editors
MARC BATI
colors
With special thanks to Anthea Schackleton
and
Starwatcher Graphics

catalan communications
new york

comcat comics
Graphic Novels

SWORD & SORCERY COLLECTION
The Magic Crystal

Other Books in This Series
Jean «Moebius» Giraud
&
Marc Bati
THE MAGIC CRYSTAL
AURELYS'S SECRET

Other Books by Jean «Moebius» Giraud
YOUNG BLUEBERRY Series
(with Jean-Michel Charlier)

1: BLUEBERRY'S SECRET
2: A YANKEE NAMED BLUEBERRY
3: THE BLUE COATS

> *"The Island of the Unicorn exists.*
> *It is the Secret Garden*
> *of our World."*
>
> *Marc Bati*

ISLAND OF THE UNICORN™
ISBN 0-87416-084-7

Story & art © 1988
Jean Giraud & Marc Bati

First worldwide book publication of
«Sur l'île de la licorne» by
Dargaud Editeur, 1988

Worldwide publishing and serialization rights
Dargaud Editeur

English language edition
© 1990 Catalan Communications

Afterword
© 1990 Bati

Published by Catalan Communications
43 East 19th Street
New York NY 10003
All Rights Reserved.
No part of this book may be printed or
reproduced in any manner whatsoever,
whether mechanical or electronic,
without the written permission
of the authors and the publisher.
All prominent characters appearing
in this book and their distinct
likenesses are a trademark of
Jean Giraud and Marc Bati.

First Comcat Comics Edition
February 1990

10 9 8 7 6 5 4 3 2 1

Depósito Legal: 39-464/89
PRINTED IN SPAIN

Write to us for a free catalogue.

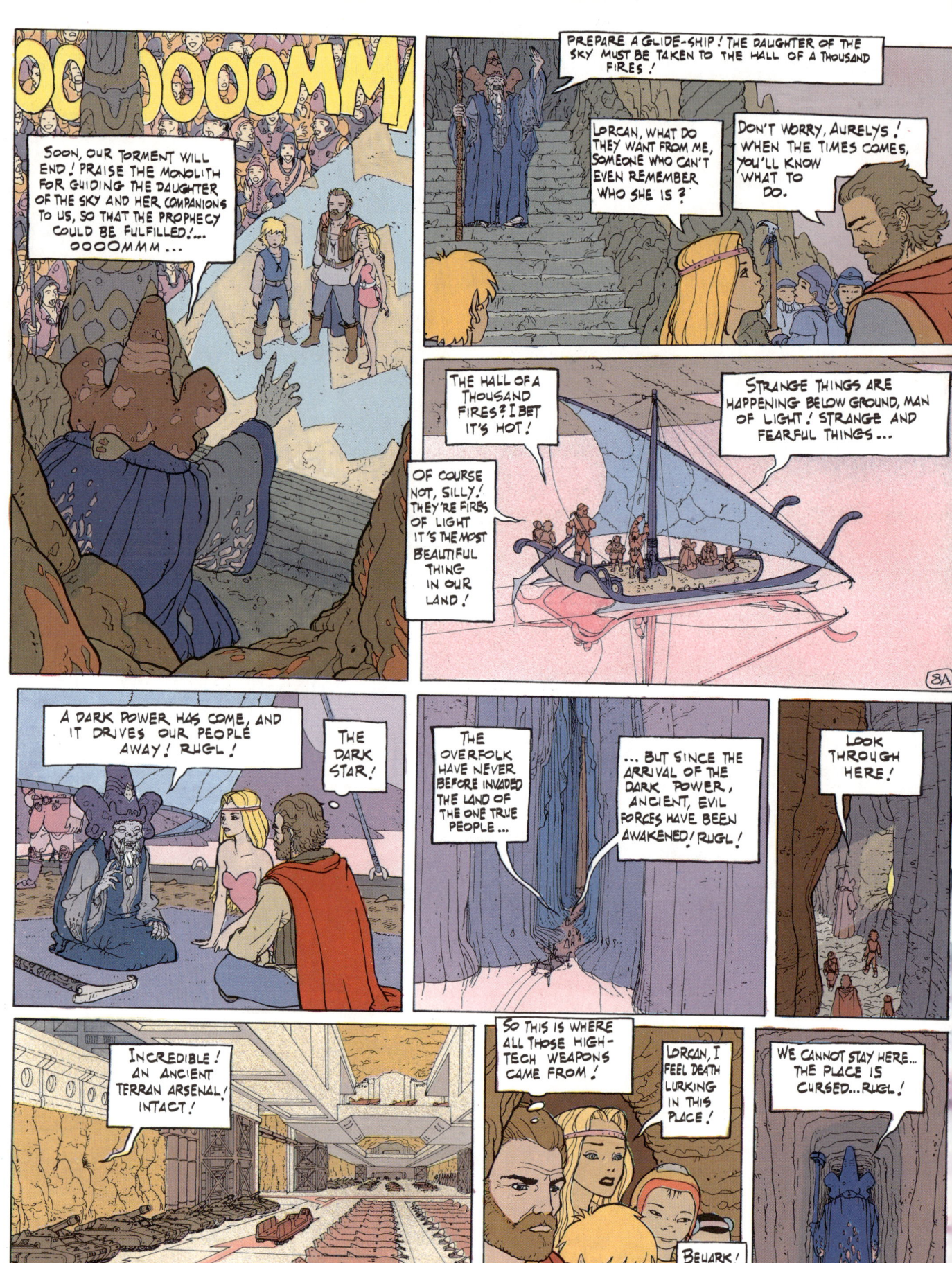

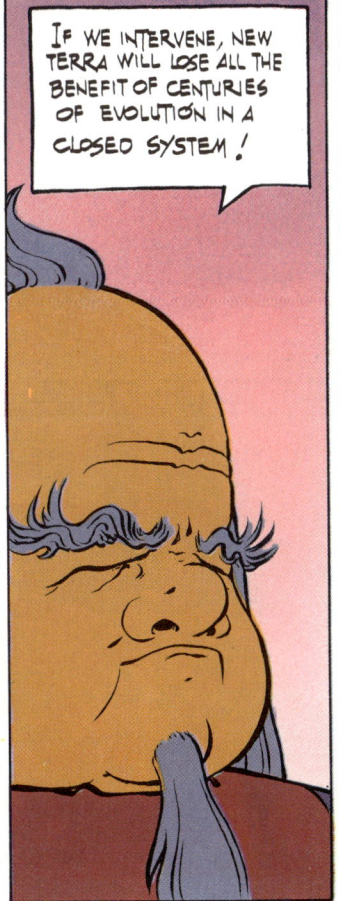

MEANWHILE...

I'VE ALREADY TRIED THIS WAY...

I SHOULD'VE BEEN OUT OF HERE AGES AGO! WHY CAN'T I FIND THE EXIT?

THAT MIND-BLAST TOOK A LOT OUT OF MY ESP POWERS...

IN THE KINGDOM OF THE NORTH...

HIGH LORD! AN ARMY FROM THE GREAT MIDDLE KINGDOM HAS CROSSED OUR BORDERS! THEY'RE UNSTOPPABLE!

BY TAMBOR! WHAT'S GOING ON?!

IN THE EAST...

...THEIR WEAPONS ARE INVINCIBLE! THEY COMMAND THE LIGHTNING!

GRUNGE!

IN THE SOUTH...

...AND THAT IS WHAT'S HAPPENING ON NEW TERRA, O, ELDERS OF AVALONIA!

INCREDIBLE!

THE GREAT COUNCIL OF AVALONIA...
THE PLANET WAS QUIETLY EVOLVING ALONG SOUND, PEACEFUL LINES, WHEN CHAOS ERUPTED!
BUT WASN'T IT EQUIPPED WITH A CRYSTAL NETWORK TO AVOID THIS KIND OF ACCIDENT?
PRECISELY, ARDON! IT SEEMS THAT THE NETWORK HAS BEEN TAMPERED WITH!
THIS REMINDS ME OF THE SATONARVIS CRISIS, IN THE TWELFTH GALAXY, EIGHT THOUSAND YEARS AGO...
YOU'RE MORE RIGHT THAN YOU SUSPECT, UTMAR! WHAT WE HAVE HERE IS AN INFILTRATION OF NEW TERRA'S CONTINUUM BY A BETA-TYPE ENTITY!
COME ON! WE ALL KNOW HOW TO CONTROL SUCH ENTITIES! THAT'S THE JOB OF THE PLANETARY MONITOR. WHAT'S HE DOING?
AH, BUT THIS IS NOT MERELY SOME WEAK, MISERABLE DEMON FROM THE EIGHTH CIRCLE! THIS IS THE DARK STAR HERSELF!
THE DARK STAR! BY THE GREAT POWERS! SHE HAS RETURNED!
WE LAST FOUGHT HER SEVERAL EONS AGO, DURING THE WAR OF THE EIGHT SUNS OF AMADORUNE. SHE PROVED SHE WAS ABLE TO INFLICT CONSIDERABLE DAMAGE TO A PLANET!
WE NEEDED THE COMBINED STRENGTH OF FOUR CELESTIAL LEGIONS TO DRIVE HER AWAY!
AND THREE OF THE EIGHT SUNS BURN NO MORE!

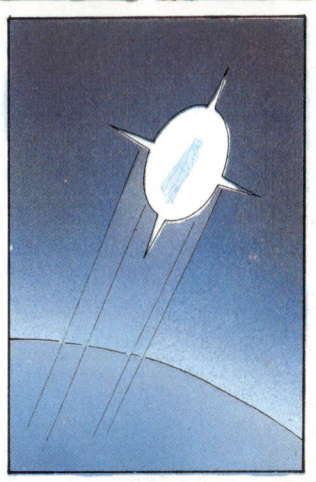

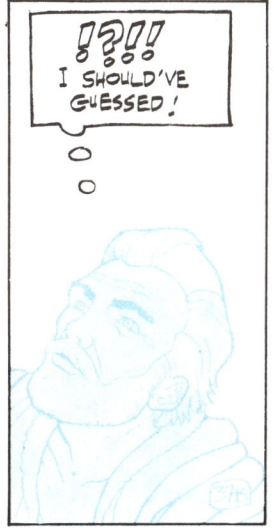

- I PROPOSE CALLING THE PLANETARY MONITOR FOR AN UPDATED REPORT AT ONCE!
- SECONDED!
- APPROVED!
- AT THAT INSTANT...
- ANOTHER DEAD END...
- IT'S AS IF A POWER SUPERIOR TO MINE WAS FORCING ME TO GO IN CIRCLES!
- BY ALTAIR! A CALL!
- HAIL, MONITOR LORCAN!
- WELCOME TO THE COUNCIL OF AVALONIA!
- WE'VE BEEN STUDYING THE SITUATION ON NEW TERRA...
- AND IT SEEMS THAT THINGS ARE GETTING OUT OF CONTROL...
- WHAT EXACTLY IS GOING ON?
- AS YOU PROBABLY KNOW, ELDERS, THE DARK STAR NOW CONTROLS A LARGE PORTION OF THE PLANET. SHE SUCCEEDED IN CAPTURING ME, AND I'VE BEEN TRYING TO ESCAPE, BUT SO FAR IN VAIN...
- THAT IS STRANGE. WITH YOUR POWERS, YOU SHOULD BE ABLE TO EASILY EVADE A BETA-TYPE ENTITY, NO MATTER HOW STRONG...
- ONLY THE NEW TERRANS SHOULD BE SUBJECT TO HER EVIL INFLUENCE. COULD THERE BE OTHER POWERS AT PLAY HERE?
- I SENSE AN UNEXPECTED GUEST, WHO MIGHT VERY WELL ANSWER THAT LAST QUESTION...
- INDEED! INDEED! THIS EXPLAINS IT ALL!
- !?!! I SHOULD'VE GUESSED!

39

ELDERS OF AVALONA, WE ARE THE "URSAMA"

WE TOOK THIS VISIBLE FORM SO THAT YOU WOULD HEAR OUR VOICE

A WORLD MIND!

NEW TERRA'S PROTECTOR SPIRIT!

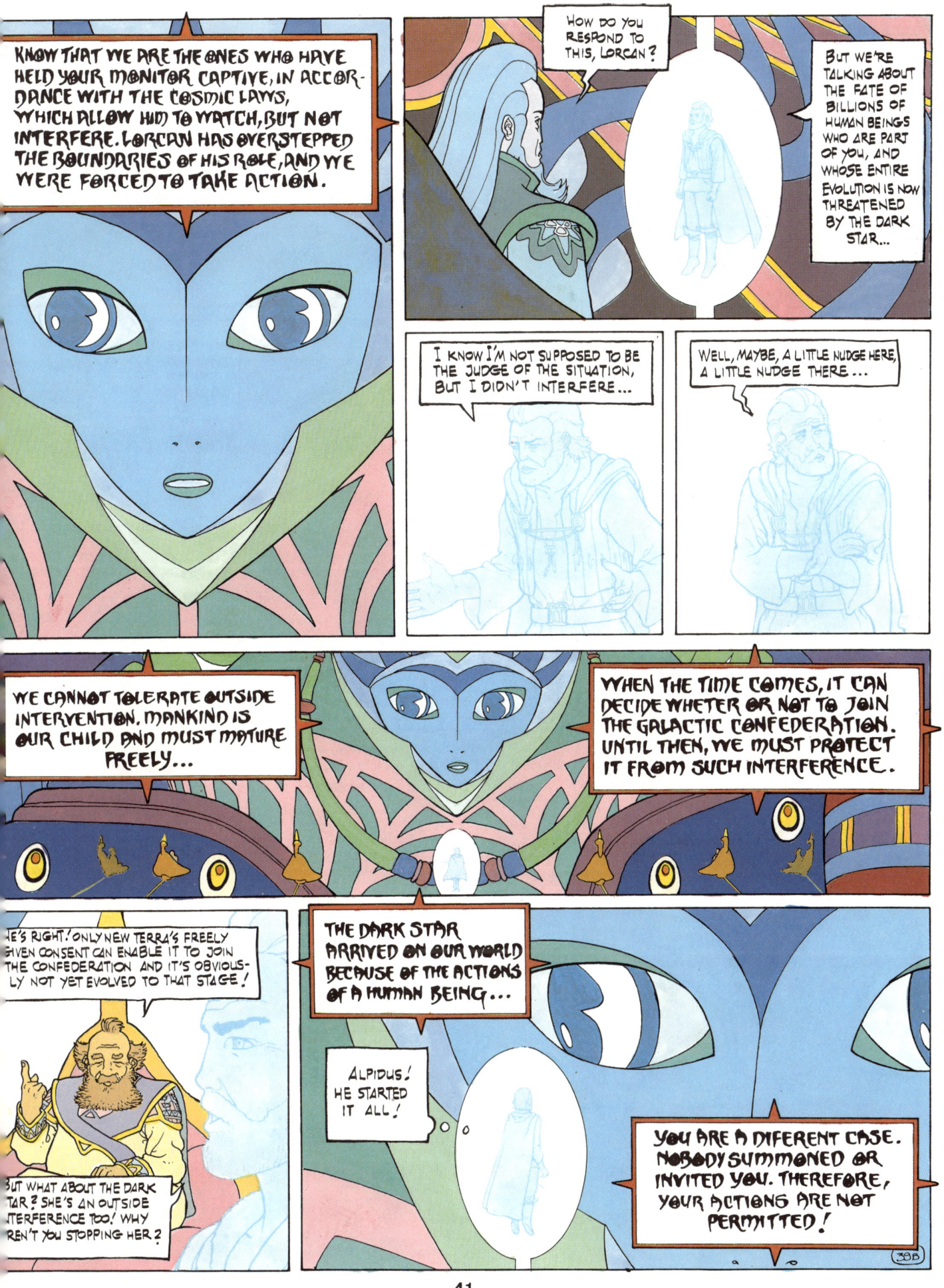

KNOW THAT WE ARE THE ONES WHO HAVE HELD YOUR MONITOR CAPTIVE, IN ACCORDANCE WITH THE COSMIC LAWS, WHICH ALLOW HIM TO WATCH, BUT NOT INTERFERE. LORCAN HAS OVERSTEPPED THE BOUNDARIES OF HIS ROLE, AND WE WERE FORCED TO TAKE ACTION.

HOW DO YOU RESPOND TO THIS, LORCAN?

BUT WE'RE TALKING ABOUT THE FATE OF BILLIONS OF HUMAN BEINGS WHO ARE PART OF YOU, AND WHOSE ENTIRE EVOLUTION IS NOW THREATENED BY THE DARK STAR...

I KNOW I'M NOT SUPPOSED TO BE THE JUDGE OF THE SITUATION, BUT I DIDN'T INTERFERE...

WELL, MAYBE, A LITTLE NUDGE HERE, A LITTLE NUDGE THERE...

WE CANNOT TOLERATE OUTSIDE INTERVENTION. MANKIND IS OUR CHILD AND MUST MATURE FREELY...

WHEN THE TIME COMES, IT CAN DECIDE WHETER OR NOT TO JOIN THE GALACTIC CONFEDERATION. UNTIL THEN, WE MUST PROTECT IT FROM SUCH INTERFERENCE.

HE'S RIGHT! ONLY NEW TERRA'S FREELY GIVEN CONSENT CAN ENABLE IT TO JOIN THE CONFEDERATION AND IT'S OBVIOUSLY NOT YET EVOLVED TO THAT STAGE!

THE DARK STAR ARRIVED ON OUR WORLD BECAUSE OF THE ACTIONS OF A HUMAN BEING...

ALPIDUS! HE STARTED IT ALL!

BUT WHAT ABOUT THE DARK STAR? SHE'S AN OUTSIDE INTERFERENCE TOO! WHY AREN'T YOU STOPPING HER?

YOU ARE A DIFERENT CASE. NOBODY SUMMONED OR INVITED YOU. THEREFORE, YOUR ACTIONS ARE NOT PERMITTED!

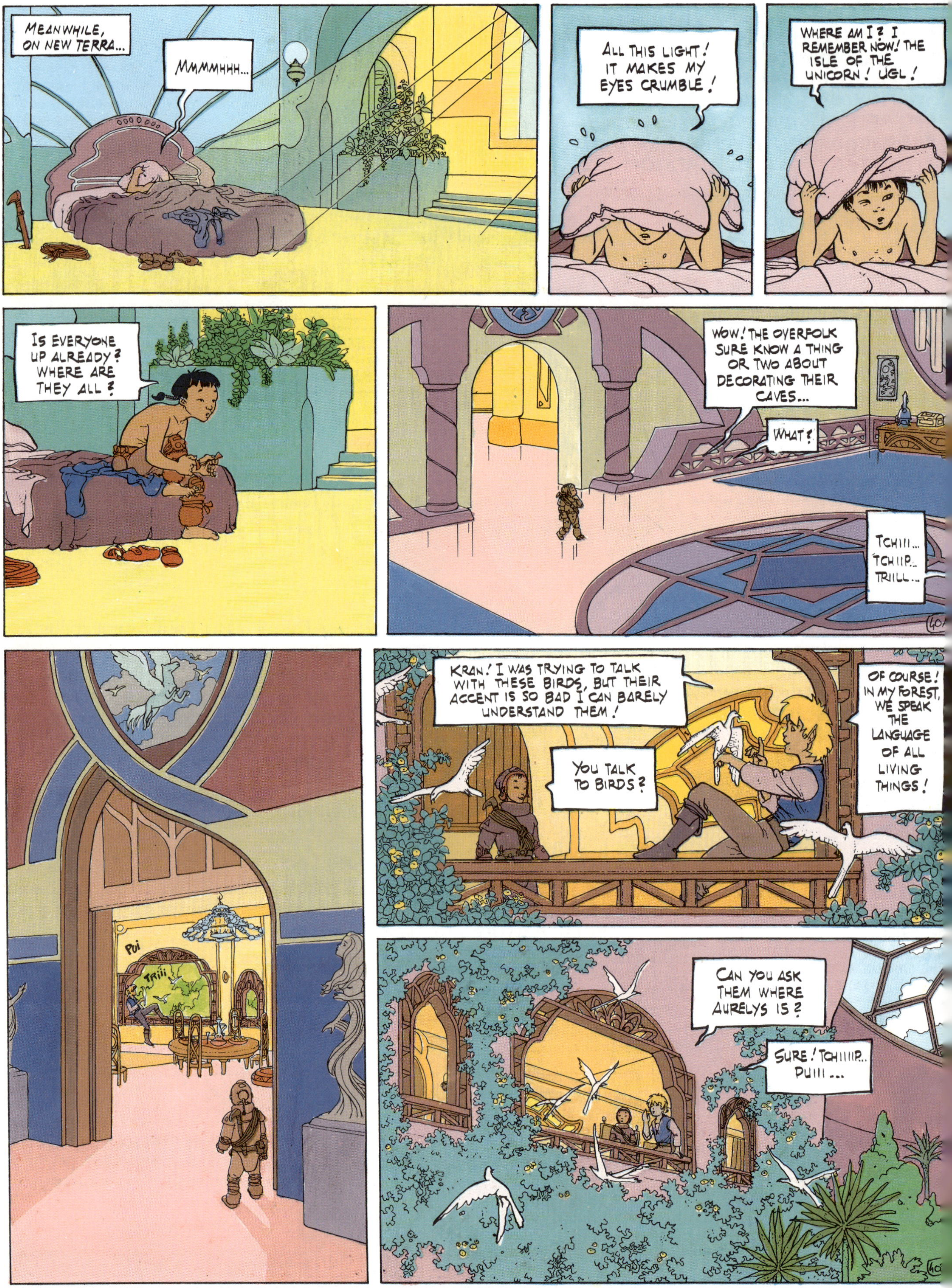
MEANWHILE, ON NEW TERRA...
MMMMHHH...
ALL THIS LIGHT! IT MAKES MY EYES CRUMBLE!
WHERE AM I? I REMEMBER NOW! THE ISLE OF THE UNICORN! UGL!
IS EVERYONE UP ALREADY? WHERE ARE THEY ALL?
WOW! THE OVERFOLK SURE KNOW A THING OR TWO ABOUT DECORATING THEIR CAVES...
WHAT?
TCHIII... TCHIIP... TRILL...
Pui
Triii
KRAN! I WAS TRYING TO TALK WITH THESE BIRDS, BUT THEIR ACCENT IS SO BAD I CAN BARELY UNDERSTAND THEM!
YOU TALK TO BIRDS?
OF COURSE! IN MY FOREST, WE SPEAK THE LANGUAGE OF ALL LIVING THINGS!
CAN YOU ASK THEM WHERE AURELYS IS?
SURE! TCHIIIIP... PUIII...

ARE THEY FLYING AWAY?
NO! THEY'RE LEADING US TO HER! LET'S FOLLOW THEM! HURRY!
I'VE LOST THEM!
THERE!
COME CLOSER! WE WERE WAITING FOR YOU!
41A
TELL ME, UNICORN, LAST NIGHT, WHEN WE SAW YOU, THAT WASN'T A DREAM, WAS IT?
I DON'T THINK SO, ALTOR, OTHERWISE WE BOTH HAD THE SAME DREAM!
INDEED, IT WAS NO DREAM. THE DARK STAR'S EVIL INFLUENCE WAS ATTEMPTING TO SAP YOUR STRENGTH, AND I HAD TO DRIVE IT AWAY!
BUT THAT IS IN THE PAST. NOW, WE MUST TALK ABOUT YOUR DEPARTURE...
WE'RE LEAVING ALREADY? WHY?
WE'RE GOING TO GO AND FREE LORCAN, AREN'T WE?
NO! THERE IS A MORE IMPORTANT TASK FOR YOU TO ACCOMPLISH...
DON'T WORRY! LORCAN'S PRETTY RESOURCEFUL FOR AN OVERFOLK!
MEANWHILE...
41B

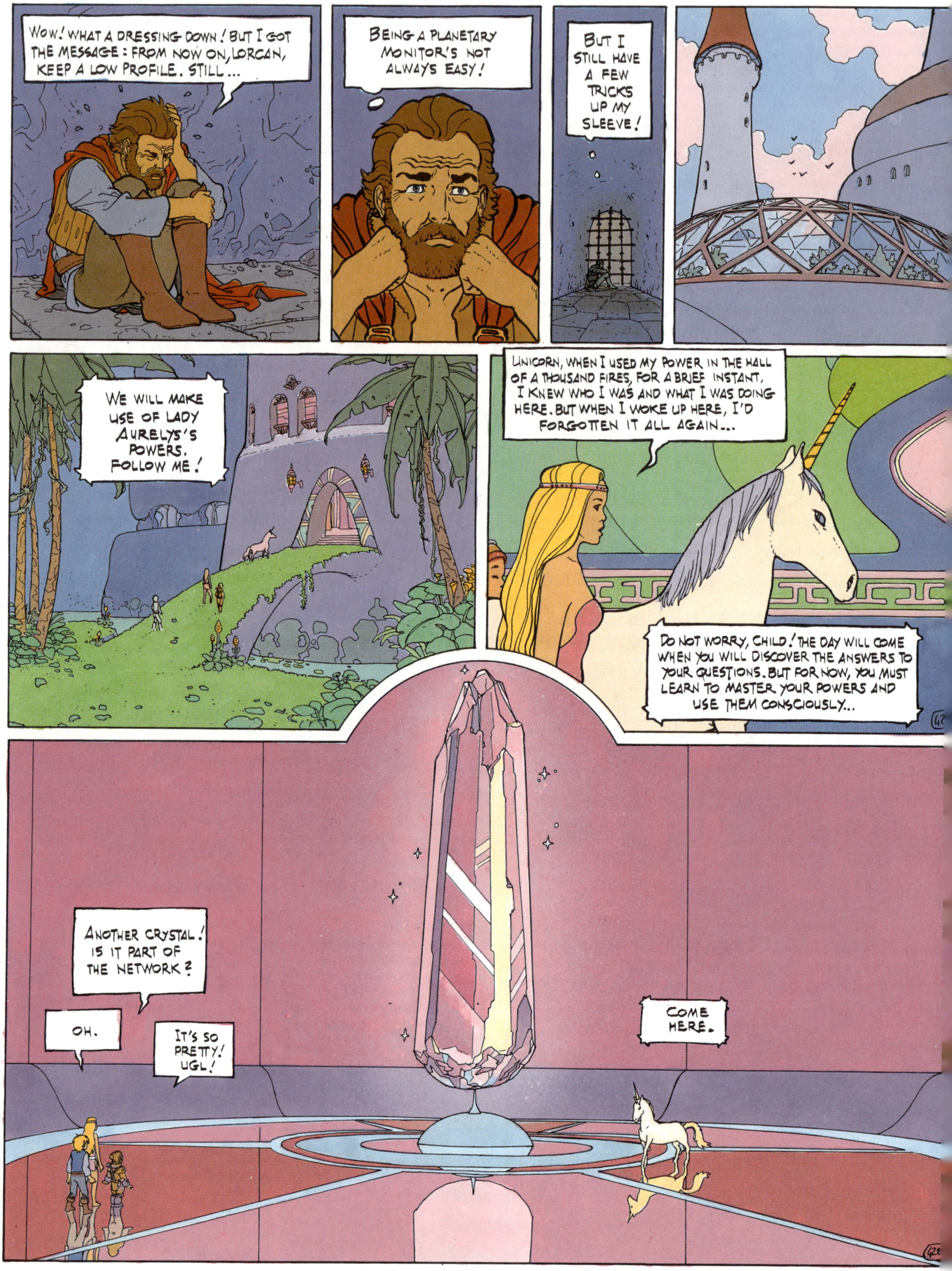
WOW! WHAT A DRESSING DOWN! BUT I GOT THE MESSAGE: FROM NOW ON, LORCAN, KEEP A LOW PROFILE. STILL...
BEING A PLANETARY MONITOR'S NOT ALWAYS EASY!
BUT I STILL HAVE A FEW TRICKS UP MY SLEEVE!
WE WILL MAKE USE OF LADY AURELYS'S POWERS. FOLLOW ME!
UNICORN, WHEN I USED MY POWER IN THE HALL OF A THOUSAND FIRES, FOR A BRIEF INSTANT, I KNEW WHO I WAS AND WHAT I WAS DOING HERE. BUT WHEN I WOKE UP HERE, I'D FORGOTTEN IT ALL AGAIN...
DO NOT WORRY, CHILD! THE DAY WILL COME WHEN YOU WILL DISCOVER THE ANSWERS TO YOUR QUESTIONS. BUT FOR NOW, YOU MUST LEARN TO MASTER YOUR POWERS AND USE THEM CONSCIOUSLY...
ANOTHER CRYSTAL! IS IT PART OF THE NETWORK?
OH.
IT'S SO PRETTY! UGL!
COME HERE.

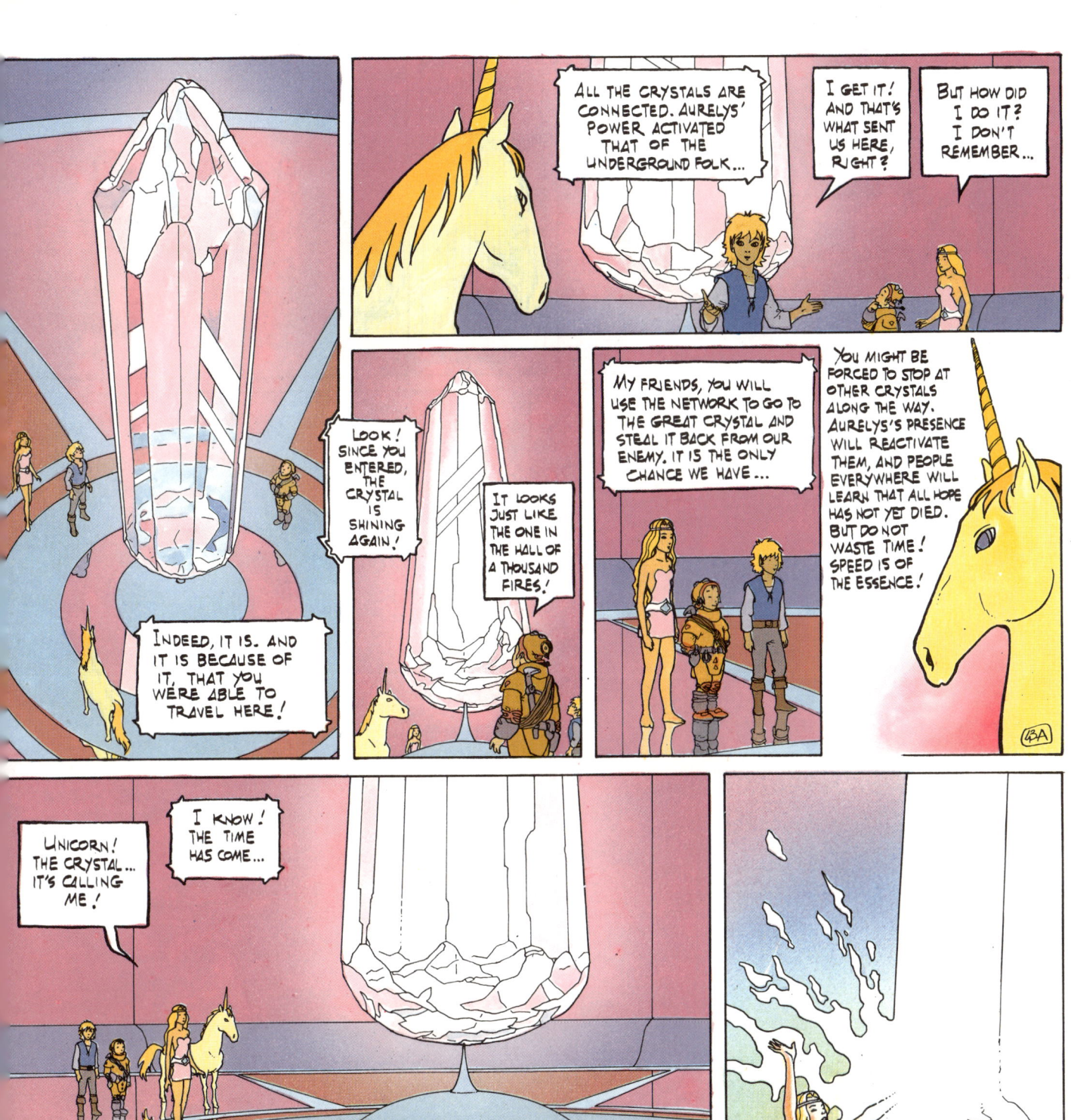

| All the crystals are connected. Aurelys' power activated that of the underground folk... | I get it! And that's what sent us here, right? | But how did I do it? I don't remember... |

Look! Since you entered, the crystal is shining again!

It looks just like the one in the hall of a thousand fires!

Indeed, it is. And it is because of it, that you were able to travel here!

My friends, you will use the network to go to the great crystal and steal it back from our enemy. It is the only chance we have...

You might be forced to stop at other crystals along the way. Aurelys's presence will reactivate them, and people everywhere will learn that all hope has not yet died. But do not waste time! Speed is of the essence!

Unicorn! The crystal... it's calling me!

I know! The time has come...

45

GO! JOIN HER!

END OF BOOK TWO.

NEXT BOOK: AURELYS'S SECR

AFTERWORD

MARC BATI

In the shade of the great coconut palms... Not very far from the pure, white, sandy beach delineating the deep, blue waters of the lagoon... In a small artist's studio built between the great Tahitian trees...

Yes, it is on a *motu* of Bora-Bora —the term used by the natives for the narrow coral bands which surround the central island— that I have chosen to live — and to draw *The Island of the Unicorn*.

But do not think that I live the life of a Robinson Crusoe, alone, dressed in rags, cut off from the rest of the world. On the contrary, my little island which was once a wilderness paradise, has since become home to a community of about fifty other people. They, like myself, are artists, psychic researchers, explorers of the mind, who have all chosen to live and work together, and form a cosmic study group, now called *Galacteus*.

I try to make my life one of harmony with a beautiful, yet unspoiled, natural corner of the Earth. Living amidst other creative people with open, positive minds, and being receptive to new ideas and susceptible to «inspiration,» in the ancient, esoteric, sense of the word, is also very important to me. All this is, without a doubt, one of the major factors which supports me, and shines through my work in *The Magic Crystal* series.

Its fairy tale atmosphere, the quasi-magical galactic entities and their myriad of colorful worlds, the very essence of supranatural communication between men and these cosmic beings are all themes which are dear to my heart. In that respect, *The Magic Crystal* is more than a mere high fantasy adventure, it is indeed an important reflection of myself, a vital part of my spiritual life.

But as is always the case with any kind of initiatic material, the story can be read on several levels. One may hopefully enjoy the simple pleasure of following Lorcan and Altor, and their companions, in their series of adventures, laugh at the humor, thrill at the dangers, without being aware of the message hidden therein. There are keys which are only accessible to those who truly desire to open certain doors.

Indeed, if there is a real purpose, or theme, to *The Magic Crystal,* it has to do with my concern over planetary evolution and ecology. I, like many others, believe that our world is a separate, living entity, which has its own evolutive cycle, and which is not necessarily subject to the same laws as ours. Could it, itself, be a giant body, with its own awareness, but on such a gargantuan scale that it would be barely perceptible to humans? Why not?

Astronomers now tell us that worlds are born, live and die, like other living creatures, but they do this on a time scale of billions of years. They follow, not a human clock, but a cosmic one. Maybe the time has come to try to truly understand the world upon which we live...

If all this seems strange and confusing to you, try to find a Unicorn to enlighten you. Unicorns are the repository of all knowledge sacred. They know everything. If you are among those who can hear the truths they can tell you, then, they will answer...

Marc Bati
Bora-Bora, September 1989